I0748022

The Extraordinary Life of Francis Wonder

The Extraordinary
Life of
Francis Wonder

Jake Pearson

Copyright © Jake Pearson 2025
The moral rights of the author have been asserted.

www.1889books.co.uk
ISBN: 978-1-915045-47-8

Contents

1

The Childhood of Francis Wonder

It began on March 5th. Theodore F. Wonder and Margret Shelly Wonder, Francis Wonder's parents, engaged in sexual relations for the first and last times in their lives. It was their wedding night. That is not to say that their desire for one another, and certainly not their love for one another, waned in the intervening years. In fact, they loved each other truly and completely from the moment their eyes first met, until the moment they died together ninety-eight years later. It was just that the physical act of love did not interest them, much in the same way that some people prefer not to watch television, or that some people could go their whole lives without once finishing a Dostoyevsky novel, so it was that Theodore and Margret Wonder chose never again to indulge in making physical love. They did so on this occasion for two simple reasons, to officially consummate their marriage, and to conceive their son. Exactly nine months later, Francis was born.

It could not be said that Francis Wonder's parents were the most traditional care-givers. In fact, some might have gone so far as to call them down-right eccentric, but they ensured Francis never wanted for food, warmth or shelter, and perhaps more importantly, they taught him the value of living for one's self.

Theodore F. Wonder was a would-be aristocrat. His clothes were pompous, even for the time, and he always donned the very best cologne and Oxford shoes. Theodore, however, was sadly lacking in the two vital departments that are perhaps the bedrocks of aristocracy, namely wealth and status. To put it mildly, Theodore Wonder was broke, and his only "connections" were his drinking companions at the local café – suffice to say not the usual hangout for the country's leading aristocrats. But Theodore Wonder was not to be deterred, for he believed true aristocracy came from the soul, not the wallet.

Given Francis Wonder's father's refusal to work – not through idleness it may be added, but out of principle and pride – the earning of money fell directly on the shoulders of Francis's mother, Margret, a load she bore with remarkable resilience and glee, for Margret was incredibly proud of her husband's aristocratic stature and strove intently to maintain the reputation she believed her family held in society.

To keep the Wonders in clothes, Margret worked three jobs; she was the village midwife, a part-time fortune teller, and the local blacksmith. She carried all her equipment in a large monogrammed (though not to her initials), faux-leather holdall. Though, unawares as to the sensitivities of others around her as Margret often was, as she unloaded the contents of her holdall piece by piece in front of the pregnant women, very few actually made it to the forceps conscious, such was their shock at seeing Margret casually remove and place before them a pack of neatly tied tarot cards, followed by a gleaming anvil.

It was these stark parallels between mother and father that birthed Francis Wonder's ability to complete tasks with the utmost ease, without ever really realising he was undertaking them. He could daydream the afternoon away whilst simultaneously taking care of all his chores and duties.

A unique and, some would say, vital skill that Francis had in his armoury, though it persisted to rub people up the wrong way.

Francis's school days meandered along with a relative lack of eventfulness, he himself conscious of the fact that these hours spent between the school walls would serve no use later in life, nor would they interest him.

It was not that Francis was vehemently against school, he was ambivalent to the extreme, and he rarely showed any signs of disdain for any member of staff or any of the things they tried to teach him. In fact, Francis was a downright studious student, polite and impressive, though not all the teachers shared the same opinion of the child. He split the faculty down the middle, half believing him to be an incredibly inspired young man, while the other half thought him bordering on dim.

The questions Francis asked his teachers were not like the questions the other children asked. They were not questions that could be answered directly, for though they were not questions from another world, per se, they were not necessarily questions that can be clearly grasped in this world, or at least it should be said, in what we understand to be this world.

And if Francis's questions left the teachers somewhat at a loss, then his answers often caused downright bewilderment.

His mathematics teacher in particular was often kept awake for many nights thinking of Francis Wonder and his answers to even the simplest equations. For you see, Francis's answers would always differ to the rest of the class, but they would rarely be wrong. That is not to say, however, that the rest of the class was wrong, just that both were right in different ways. There was no logical explanation for this, particularly given the basic principles of mathematics, yet reading through Francis's workings, it was plain to see that his conclusions were in fact correct; simply, two and two could in fact often equal more than just four, and sometimes less. In fact, Francis's teacher soon came to understand that rarely did it ever equal four.

Given how little importance Francis Wonder attributed to his schooling days, however, these are not times that necessitate a great deal of narrating, and so we shall move swiftly on to a period of much more pertinence.

2

War

By the time Francis Wonder has turned eighteen, war had broken out across Europe, and being a fit and able young male, he was conscripted to fight for his country.

Francis had little interest in war, but just as with school, he understood the necessity it would play in his life, so he buckled down and worked at becoming an adequate soldier.

Francis's best friend in the army was a man of similar age, named Jacques DuTroit. The two trained at the academy together for six months. They shared a bunk bed and a disdain for violence. As luck would have it the two were deployed to the same unit after finishing their training, sent to the trenches to defend their country at close quarters.

Jacques died on his first day in the trenches, the very morning he arrived in fact. A speculative bullet fired from behind enemy lines, more a reminder they were there than anything else, struck Francis's friend in the centre of his forehead as he took an inquisitive peak over the top of the trench. The events of that morning tested more than ever before Francis's usually peaceful constitution.

This is not a war novel, nor is it a history book, so the details of the war itself will be concise, necessary, and frankly, more often than not, entirely inaccurate. The war itself is not of any real significance, it is merely the backdrop of this period of Francis's life.

After the death of Jacques, Francis settled quietly into life in the trenches, keeping mainly to himself. He was an eccentric sort, but he was generally well-liked by all who knew him. Though he was never short of friendly words or invitations to various evenings playing cards, Francis struggled to keep himself from making too many deep connections with his unfortunately doomed fellow soldiers.

It was not that Francis was psychic as such, he had no real way of knowing what would ultimately happen to his section when, two years later, they would all perish due to a mishap with a hand grenade. But when Francis looked at his fellow troops he could see through them, not clearly, but they appeared faint, opaque to him, and he took this to mean impending death.

Fortunately for Francis, he would have left the section by the time the grenade pin was stealthily plucked from the corporal's belt by a particularly brave magpie. Given no one had noticed the thievery, it came as quite a surprise to all involved when the corporal, and then the troops themselves, suddenly exploded.

As was the case for most involved, the war took its toll on Francis. His sunny disposition became increasingly downcast, the clouds of sorrow hanging heavy all around. The smell of death seemed to have burrowed its way into his nostrils and set up camp, while the sound of death, incessant and protruding, now lived in the innermost part of his ear canals.

War bears no victors, that much is undoubtedly true. There are small wins followed by mass defeat. This was clear to Francis from the onset, but even he didn't realise how much evil lived underneath the soil of the earth, seeping its way into the souls of the men he called his allies, as well as the men he was told to regard as enemies.

War is never uneventful, but by paradox, the constant eventfulness created a mundane dullness. Just as a farmer might plough the same field for his entire life, or an office worker might indulge in the same monotonous task day in day out, so too does death and destruction become just another uninteresting daily occurrence during wartime.

It happened almost a year to the day that Francis had first arrived at the trench. It was a cool, summer evening, clear skies and an odd tranquillity, and Francis was on patrol as night watchman. It was a duty Francis didn't mind all too much. Unlike most of the men, he had little trouble sleeping in the day, so he was more than happy to bear the lion's share of the night shift. Another reason for his overt acceptance of the duty was the free time it allowed him to work on his javelin technique.

The one thing Francis did thank his schooling days for was his introduction to javelin, a pastime he became equally devoted to and proficient in. He set a new record at his school for distance in his first year competing, a record he broke every year thereafter.

Unwilling to allow his form to become sluggish, Francis used these comparatively calm nights to simulate the act of throwing a javelin, using his bayonetted rifle as a substitute.

As a rule Francis would use the free space, with the vast majority of the men asleep in their bunks, to make his run. 10 sprint steps followed by three crossover steps. He would then simulate the release of the javelin.

On this particular night, however, such was the force of his run and thrust, he struggled to maintain hold of his rifle and could only hold his breath as it sailed over the top of the trench and into no man's land. Suddenly, out of the strange silence of the night reverberated a shot.

A few of the men gathered around Francis, who eventually lifted his head above the trench. Before him he saw three enemy soldiers faced down in the mud.

As it turned out, the enemy had enlisted three specialists – men renowned to both sides as the very best in their field – to make their way across no man's land under the cover of darkness. Armed with enough explosives to wipe out a small city, they were to exterminate, along with themselves, it seemed, the entirety of Francis's platoon.

Unfortunately for them, given Francis's exceptional skill when it came to throwing a javelin, the point of the bayonet landed squarely in the chest of the leader of the triplet, and as it lodged there, the force with which it was thrown had caused the rifle to fire. Given the three men had been stealthily making their way across no man's land in single file, so as to create the smallest target possible, the shot from the gun had travelled through the first man, through the second, and nestled itself neatly in the heart of the third.

Francis had foiled the most daring plot the enemy had to offer and was unanimously hailed a hero.

No amount of explanation on Francis's side could persuade his commanding officer he was not the enemy-slayer he was being made out to be, and, rightly or wrongly, Francis Wonder was awarded a medal for gallantry and granted early leave from the army.

3

Eremos

Such is the case for many men returning from war, the adjustment back into normal society proved a difficult proposition for Francis Wonder. Never a person completely at ease with the way of the world even beforehand, things now seemed so desolate and uninspired, so lacking in meaning and full of vehemence and dystopia.

Life back with his parents seemed unfulfilling, and particularly given his "hero" status among the locals, forgetting the events of the past few years proved increasingly difficult. Francis knew he must move on.

Theodore and Margret were hardly surprised by their son's announcement, as he informed his parents of his intentions to travel the globe in search of a place he felt more at ease.

Never having been in the business of wing clipping, Francis's parents offered ample encouragement and a small amount of spending money to help their only child on his journey. Francis set out the following morning.

Francis's travels were extensive, meandering to the far ends of the earth in search of like-minded individuals, of a different existence, one he had always felt inside himself since the moment of his birth.

For the most part, however, Francis's journey provided him with little else other than the same despondency that he had struggled to shrug off since returning from the trenches. His time spent in large cities, modern metropolises teeming with skyscrapers and egotism, showed Francis how self-centred mankind really had become. Greed and corruption swept along every street as fleetingly as a discarded crisp packet, while happiness sank into the gutters to keep company with the countless homeless citizens. Egos were so inflated that Francis was often surprised when mankind did not simply float off into the atmosphere, their greed the helium that propelled them ever higher, until eventually they burst on impact with the sun, the torn remains of a human balloon falling softly back to earth, to embed itself into the soil and begin the whole human cycle once more.

Bemused by the life led by so many in these metropolitan times, Francis ventured as far as he could from civilised society, even so far as spending time on remote islands amongst tribespeople and 'savages.'

Though wholly different from the city-men, the basic fundamentals remained, seemingly engrained in the species somehow. Though the greed was not for money, it still existed, perhaps even to a more extreme extent, while the desire for power led to bloodshed the likes of which Francis had hoped he would never again have to witness, curdling his insides and bringing back vivid memories of Jacques DuTroit and his fellow soldiers. Francis's despondency only intensified.

To say his entire travels did little to increase Francis's faith in mankind, however, would be to overlook the place that he came closest to calling a home. By sheer chance, while travelling through Eremos, a desert so full of solitude and wilderness, Francis stumbled upon a small group of people wearing thick, wool ponchos, the hoods so large as to cover their entire faces. They each had a mole-like quality, hunched over to keep the whipping sands out of their eyes. These people, it turned out, were the sole inhabitants of Eremos, the only six people who had ever managed to adapt to the harsh climate and destitute lifestyle that one had to suffer living in a place like this.

The six were a family; a father, mother, their daughter and her three children. They also had a dog called Nimble. Nimble was a greyhound, slender and noble and loyal to a fault. He had mistakenly stepped off a tourist bus at the far east of the desert and, having been separated from his original owners, had come across the desert dwellers in his search for food. The family took Nimble in, taught him to hunt desert rats, and made him his very own poncho.

After introducing himself and learning all he could about the family's history, Francis spent the best part of six months living in Eremos, adapting most impressively to the lifestyle.

He became great friends with the father of the family, and Nimble took an extreme liking to Francis. For the most part, he was happy.

As the harsh summer drew on, though, it became clear the father's strength was waning. He was no longer a young man, and the decades living in this most desolate of places had rendered his body frail and unstable.

Francis, the father and Nimble had gone out in search of food. After a short period of walking, the father

12

stopped and took a seat in the sand. He patted the ground either side of him, beckoning Francis and Nimble to take a seat, which they both did.

"I'm dying, Francis." The father spoke in hushed tones.

"My body is too old to sustain itself on what we have here."

At this point he removed a fresh piece of meat from the inside of his poncho and fed it to Nimble.

"Surely," Francis implored, "Nimble could make do with a little less food if it meant you had enough to go on living? Why do you treat him as some sort of superior being?"

"Is he not?" The father took a short pause. "Man's intelligence is superior to that of an animal, but man thinks that equates to superiority."

Francis's face made an involuntary motion, perhaps bracing against the whipping sands, perhaps against what he could feel rising up inside him.

"Intelligence is but one quality," the father continued. "Yet it is the one we judge everything by, which is a handy coincidence for mankind given it is the only quality in which we are in fact superior. Were we to judge such things on loyalty, devotion, happiness, or perhaps the ability to love without condition or prejudice, who in fact would you call the superior being?

God is love. By most religious texts that is true. But humans cannot give love purely, they cannot love without conception or condition. Dogs, however, know no other way to love. Whether I treat Nimble with love or contempt, whether I feed him or not, whether I give him shelter or leave him out in the unthinkable conditions, he will still love unconditionally. So then, Francis, who is closer to God, he, or I?"

Francis stared intently and knew then that the father was right.

"I need to ask a favour of you," the father told Francis. "Nimble cannot stay here after I am gone. My family cannot fend for themselves and keep him fed. Will you take him with you?"

Francis managed only a solitary nod.

After saying this the father took one final piece of meat from his poncho, placed it between Nimble's teeth and stroked him behind the left ear. He then laid on his back in the sand and peacefully died.

The wind blew hard and the sand crashed against the back of Francis's poncho. As its momentum gathered the sand began to cover the father's body, and when Francis reached out to touch his friend he found only sand remaining. The father had become part of the desert, part of Eremos.

Francis took Nimble and returned to the remaining family members. He told the father's wife, his daughter and the grandchildren what had happened, and what the father had asked of him regarding the dog.

There were no hysterics from the family, not even a tear, just a solemn nod to Francis and a gentle embrace between the six of them.

This, like all events past, present and future, had already been foretold. The family could read the sand. They already knew what would pass on this day.

After spending a final evening with the family, Francis Wonder and Nimble set out early the next morning in search of pastures new. He was unspeakably sad to leave the people he knew in his heart had become a second family to him, but he knew it was time to move on.

4

How the Town of Wonder Came to Be

The arctic tern has the longest migration of any bird, travelling around fifty thousand miles per year. They do not migrate as the crow flies, however – they take a meandering path to their destination, for it is the journey, not the destination, that is the adventure, or so the bird seems to say.

Over their lifespan, these miraculous birds will travel a distance equivalent to three round trips to the moon. To Francis Wonder that seemed a little excessive.

Francis was worn out from his travels, he needed a place to rest, a place to begin to call his home, but the one constant he had discovered on his own migration was that nowhere seemed to fit quite right.

Francis decided to continue his search, but no longer was he looking for a ready-made place to settle into. Instead, Francis set off with Nimble in search of a place where he could create his own town, a place where he could rest at ease, a place where he could dream.

The journey was a long one, eleven months in total. Francis passed through more places than he knew existed, searching for what exactly he did not yet know. But he knew that he would know once he arrived.

On the first day of the twelfth month of his pilgrimage, Francis came upon a man, and the man had a raft. Francis introduced himself and asked where the raft could take him, but the man did not reply, he just grinned a toothy grin and nodded his head slightly.

Undeterred, Francis crossed the palm of the man with a coin and the man motioned for him to board the raft, which he did.

The two men and Nimble sailed, or floated, on the raft for half the day, through swampland, through thick reeds and finally out onto the clearest water Francis had ever cast his eyes upon. Carp and mackerel swam contentedly alongside the raft, looking graceful and delicious in equal measure, while the scenery surrounding, so vibrant with botanical life, took Francis's breath away.

The man steering the raft had seemingly had his breath taken away so often by these wonders he had now been rendered permanently speechless. He just grinned his toothy grin at Francis and at the river.

Eventually they reached their destination and Francis and Nimble disembarked. Half expecting the man to have dissipated into the atmosphere and to be left wondering about his actual reality, Francis turned to where the raft should have been. But there stood the man, grinning his grin and waving his hand. Francis grinned, waved back and continued forward.

It was after a short amount of travelling that Francis happened upon a sheep. It was an ordinary sheep in practically every aspect, the exception being that its fleece was the most startling white Francis Wonder had ever cast his eyes upon. The wool sparkled in the midday sun, radiating an almost evangelical glow.

It was then that Francis's attention was caught by a gentle humming sound. At first it was non-distinct, but the more Francis strained to listen, the more he could detect an undercurrent of melody.

Following the sound Francis arrived at a beehive. Exceptional in no immediately detectable way, it soon became apparent, as the bees came and went from the hive, that they were most certainly buzzing in tune with each other, creating inside the hive a cacophony of sound; music even.

A sudden feeling of revelation, if revelation can in fact be called a feeling, washed over Francis. He knew then that this would be the place he must build the town of Wonder.

5

The Introduction of Magical Mert and his Spectacular Travelling Circus (and Annie)

It took time and effort, and lots of both, but after seven more months Francis Wonder had built himself the beginnings of a small town.

It is impossible to truly understand the town of Wonder without ever having visited. Thus it would be impossible to relay in simple terms exactly how it was that Francis was able to single-handedly build a small town in seven months. But like everything else that occurred in Wonder, explanation was never considered necessary.

It took a little time for word to get out about the town, but after another six months had passed the community was beginning to flourish.

The first inhabitants, aside from Francis of course, were all sixty-eight members of Magical Mert's Spectacular Traveling Circus.

This gang of acrobats, lion tamers, fortune tellers, clowns, mimes, trapeze artists, sword swallowers, fire eaters, tightrope walkers, ventriloquists, ventriloquist's dummies, to name but a few, had been on the road for the best part of twenty-five years, and had decided it was time to find a place to settle down for a while.

In truth, this was a decision made by a sub-committee of the performers, to protect the health of Mert himself, for though he would never admit it, thirty years of travelling the world with a multitude of circuses had taken its toll on his body (no one was actually sure of Mert's real age - some speculated that he had long since passed a century of years on this earth).

Mert was mild mannered, or at least mild mannered for a ring master. He had set up his own circus over two decades previously when the treatment of performers across the industry was at an all-time low. He dreamt of a circus run by performers, not accountants and entrepreneurs, and as his own circus grew, so did the number of people he would call his family members.

It wasn't Mert, however, but rather his daughter, Annie, who approached Francis in the hope that she and her large and curious family could maybe find a home in Wonder.

It was a warm spring evening and Francis was sitting outside his newly built home. Nimble was curled at his feet.

It was then that he first set eyes on Annie, emerging from the tall grass, silhouetted by the early evening sun, dipped just into the horizon.

Immediately Francis thought she was the most beautiful woman he had ever seen. She was perfectly freckled and her hair was the colour of a Japanese Maple Tree, burning a vibrant autumnal orange. Her eyes were malleable, inviting, enticing you to curl up and spend an afternoon napping in them. She emitted a soft, warm glow that brought colour and light to all surrounding her; each setting she passed through quickly gaining, and then losing, a dreamlike quality as she turned the world upside down.

She approached Francis somewhat meekly, but not through a lack of self-belief or intimidation. It was just that her proposal bore so much significance she dared not think of the consequences should Francis refuse her and her family sanctuary.

Annie lifted her head, looked Francis intently in his left eye, and began to open her mouth. But before the sound of her voice had time to work its way from her brain, down to the bottom of her stomach, back up through her diaphragm and out of her lips via her teeth, Francis himself spoke.

"Of course your family can stay," he tried to say with as little pomposity as possible.

Annie smiled a knowing smile. Not because she had anticipated Francis's anticipation, but knowing rather because in that moment time ceased presenting itself in the manner to which she had become accustomed, namely in the form of past, present and future. Annie's time had merged. Past, present and future were no longer separate notions. Just for an instant.

Annie turned and walked back over the horizon, through the tall grass and into the sun. She would return in the morning with the rest of her family, all sixty-eight of whom would become an integral part of Francis's life.

Michel brushed the sand from between his toes with a single-minded urgency, each nerve of his body scrunching awkwardly. He hated the feeling of sand between his toes.

"But sand between the toes is more than the physical." Michel's mother told him. "Sand between the toes is the tangible resonance of enjoyment, proof that today has been a good day."

Francis sat in the armchair and listened to what his wife was saying, suddenly aware that he loved this woman more than he ever thought imaginable.

"I still hate how it feels," said Michel.

Francis and Annie smiled at each other.

6

A Little About the Town

Wonder was a town like all other towns, or at least it seemed so at first, but it quickly became apparent that there was something special, something mystical, something, well, Wondrous about this place.

Butterflies were a permanent feature in Wonder, and though they might have seemed at first glance the kind of butterflies you see in any other town, if you listened carefully enough, you could hear the beat of their wings, and the wings of the butterflies in Wonder all beat in perfect unison. This gentle thrumming accounted for the percussion section of the town.

And just as Francis had previously noticed, the bees all buzzed in melodious harmony; the string section.

The birds provided the woodwind and the cats, dogs, mice, foxes, badgers and whatever other animals felt inclined to involve their vocal chords, contributed most splendidly to the brass section.

Such was the case that there was always an underlying soundtrack to life in Wonder, and who knew animals were so well versed in Rat Pack classics?

This is just a tangible, if anything in Wonder could ever in fact be considered tangible, example of the curiosities of the town. In Wonder everyone was well fed, they had water (and wine) aplenty, there was always one more house available when a new inhabitant made their way into town, and no one ever wanted for extra warmth, or more breeze in the stifling summer air. Essentially, all basic amenities were taken care of. Exactly how this was possible would be impossible to explain. Impossibilities, improbabilities, impracticalities, they were all quite possible, probable and practical in Wonder. And, what's more, no one ever questioned these things, for sometimes, the key to being happy is to be too ignorant to be unhappy.

7

Two Small People and a Party

On the evening of the second day of the circus's residency in Wonder there came a knock upon Francis's door. Having lived in the town in solitude for the past few months the sound startled him somewhat. Upon opening the door Francis saw no person, but a jack-in-the-box left on his step. Francis turned the crank for what seemed like an age - it was in fact two and a half minutes, but two and a half minutes can seem like an age when one is turning a jack-in-the-box crank on one's front doorstep. Nothing happened.

He took the box inside and left it on his armchair while he went to look for something to prise it open with.

When he returned with a screwdriver he saw that box was now on its side, and that the lid was open.

Francis approached with caution and looked inside, but it was empty. He took it in his arms and turned to sit on his armchair, so as to properly investigate the object. But before his buttocks could reach the plush pillow he heard a deafening shriek from below. Francis jumped up and swivelled his body round and as he looked upon the armchair cushion he saw two very tiny people, one man and one women.

"Watch it! You dummy!" said the little man.

The little women pinched his arm and he howled.

"Please excuse Jack," she said. "He's always grumpy after a night in the box."

Francis opened his mouth but no words exited.

"It's okay," said the little woman, "we get that a lot. My name's Jill, I'm one of the acrobats with the circus. And this is Jack, he's in the band."

"Jack and Jill…" was all that escaped Francis's lips.

"Oh yes," said Jill, "but not that Jack and Jill, goodness no."

"I'm so sick of people thinking that," said Jack. "That dummy Jack is such a nitwit. Not a day goes by that he doesn't end up at the bottom of that hill with his skull cracked open. NITWIT!"

"Jack!" Jill snapped at him.

"Anyway, sorry to drop in like this but we just came to invite you to a little party that some of the guys and girls from the circus are throwing tonight. We understand if you don't want to come, but I must tell you, our parties are pretty legendary."

"And how!" added Jack.

Francis hadn't taken in much of what had been said, but he was never one to be rude, so he graciously accepted Jack and Jill's party invitation before offering them a glass of lemonade.

And so it was that they spent the afternoon on Francis's armchair drinking lemonade and sucking on gobstoppers, talking about nothing in particular.

Jack and Jill then bade their farewell and returned to the jack-in-the-box, asking Francis politely if he could pop them back outside on the front door step for collection, which he promptly did, adding that they were welcome to come round for lemonade and gobstoppers anytime.

8

How Magnificent Mert Lost Both His Wife and His Leg in the Same Evening

Magnificent Mert was widely regarded as the most trailblazing ring master this side of the hemisphere, and not only because he could hold even the most derisive of audiences in complete captivity from the beginning of his performance until to the very last second, performing acrobatic feats, fantastical conjuring tricks and the most mesmerising lion-taming act you ever feasted your eyes upon. The reason Mert was so especially spellbinding was that he did all of this with just one leg.

Just how he came to lose his leg was, like Mert himself, a quite unbelievable story, one that Francis would learn from the Rita the Fire Eater and Saul the Human Cannonball that night at the party.

Rita and Saul had taken it upon themselves to play the role of welcoming party for Francis. They plied him with a marvellous liquid concoction, the likes of which he had never previously tasted, they encouraged him with crudités, and they smothered him with general niceties.

As grateful as Francis was for their affection, he was inwardly disappointed not to be receiving the same level of attention from Annie, who remained engaged in deep conversation with her father at the far end of the room.

Unable to avoid noticing Francis's constant glances in Annie's direction, Rita and Saul quickly realised the depths of his attraction to the girl. They thought it only fair he should know what he was getting himself into should Annie return his infatuation, so they proceeded to inform the town founder of a little background involving Mert and Annie.

"Before Mert was the Magnificent Mert," began Rita. "Before he began his long-standing relationship with circus life, Mert was a notorious gambler."

"He was known as Mert the Merciless," Saul continued the story with almost rehearsed precision.

"He was given this name due to his seeming inability to lose at cards, and for his lack of sympathy for his opponents," said Rita.

"He delighted in never leaving a penny on the table for his conquests," said Saul.

"In those days," said Rita, "he travelled with a woman named Florence, his wife. She was always present at his card games, for she was completely enthralled by the adrenaline that surged through her body when Mert would make the most ludicrous of wagers."

"He was notorious for betting the most outrageous things," said Saul. "Things like his clothes, his gold teeth, just for the hell of it."

"This one particular night," continued Rita, "Mert was in a particularly foolhardy mood."

"And by this time," Saul added, "Florence had given birth to their daughter, Annie." Francis glanced in Annie's direction; she was still engrossed in the conversation with her father.

"Annie travelled with Mert and Flo," said Rita, "and thus she was there the night Mert lost his leg."

"And his wife!" added Saul.

"The rumour in town was that a new card player would be passing through that evening, and the story went that he had never in his life lost a single hand."

"Well," Saul continued, "Mert was practically giddy with excitement. He was tired of taking money from the drunks and lowlifes at the saloon, he was desperate for a real game of cards.

"Five card draw was the game," said Rita.

"The very first hand, Mert drew two kings and two queens, and when he pulled another king on the draw he was assured of victory."

"He went all in," said Saul, "but the other fellow raised."

"Desperate for something else to bet Mert offered up his clothes and his gold teeth, as was usual practice," explained Rita.

"But the other fellow shook his head and pointed to his own leg," said Saul.

"And when Mert and Flo looked closer," said Rita, "they saw that his left leg was made out of wood."

"He then pointed to Mert's leg," said Saul.

"So confident was Mert that he instantly agreed to wager his left leg," said Rita.

"The cards were flipped and Mert laid down his full house," said Saul.

"He went to rake in the pot," said Rita, "but before he could the man with the wooden leg laid down his cards."

"A straight flush!" said Saul.

"Mert demanded they play one more hand," Rita told Frances, "but the man with wooden leg gestured that Mert the Merciless had nothing left to wager."

"That's when Mert grinned and nodded towards Florence," said Saul.

Frances was shocked, he couldn't believe someone would wager their wife in a game of five card draw. "That's awful!" he cried.

"Well," said Rita, "yes... and no."

"You see," continued Saul, "so overcome was Flo with adrenaline, before the man with the wooden leg could answer either in the affirmative or the negative, Mert's wife had leapt onto the table and sat cross-legged on top of the pot of money that remained there from the previous hand."

"Suffice to say," Rita said sufficiently, "the man with the wooden leg won the hand and Mert had to give up both his leg and his wife."

"Funny thing is," said Saul, "the man with the wooden leg and Florence fell madly in love."

"And still are to this day," added Rita.

"Yeah," said Saul, "they got married the next day and have lived happily in that same town ever since. We still see them from time to time, or at least we used to, when the circus would pass through."

"He's actually a very lovely man," said Rita. "He and Mert are quite good friends now."

Frances was dumbfounded. "And how does Annie feel about all of this," he asked.

"It's always hard to tell with Annie," said Rita. "She doesn't quite feel things like other people."

"And she's so busy caring for everyone else in the circus," Saul added, "it's almost like she doesn't have time to think about it all too much."

"But she loves her dad more than anything in the world," said Rita. "You see, it was after that night that Mert gave up gambling and took Annie and joined his first circus."

"He started as a hand," said Saul, "mainly mucking out the elephants. But it was quickly apparent how much talent he had for the business, and indeed the lifestyle."

"He devoted himself to Annie and to the circus," said Rita, "and as she grew into a hugely talented and caring young girl, so did Mert grow into the warm-hearted man he is today."

"Maybe this story paints Mert in a slightly negative light," said Saul, "but it's important you know about our past."

"But it's more important," added Rita, "that you understand that Mert is the head of this family, and is unequivocally loved and adored by every member. He is an amazing man and the most caring person I have ever met."

"I understand," said Francis.

And thus he knew that the way to Annie's heart was through her father, and through her large and spectacular family. So he set about ingratiating himself into the circus's community, a task he would relish completely.

It was a warm spring afternoon when Francis looked out towards the violet mountains in the distance. A raindrop falling on his nose had caused him to look up from his book.

The freshly laundered sheets were drying on the line and Francis rose to bring them in from the rain.

Annie caught his hand and pulled him back onto the grass next to her.

"Not yet," she whispered.

Francis laid his head back on the grass and let the droplets fall in his face. He knew that Annie loved the smell of fresh rain on the sheets.

9

How Bruce, the Smiling Scarecrow,
Arrived in Wonder

At this point in time, it was still hugely ambitious to be calling Wonder a "town." In fact, it was still, as yet, unnamed.

Granted, Francis had managed to erect himself a fairly respectable abode, but the vast majority of the circus were still living out of their travelling trailers – not that any of them minded much.

It wasn't until Bruce Fella arrived in Wonder that things really began to take shape.

The morning was awash with pastel colours, the wind bristled and the sky seemed more at one with itself than it had ever been. It was a Tuesday.

Bruce Fella, like all new inhabitants of Wonder, appeared almost prophetically in the distance, backed by the sun and emerging from the same tall grass from which Annie had first presented herself to Francis.

This was not the only entrance into Wonder, but it was the one that every inhabitant undertook when first arriving at the town, almost like the town itself was making a declaration of their entrance.

Bruce cut a striking figure, some 7 feet 9 inches tall but without the necessary "meat-on-the-bones" to properly fill out his huge frame, he gave the appearance more of an undernourished scarecrow than that of a human being – at least from a distance.

Even more striking than his physical appearance, however, was the undeniable radiation of Bruce's smile, which leapt from his face every time he lifted his straw fedora from his head – which was often.

So startlingly enthralling was his beam, in fact, that numerous townsfolk swear it was the first thing they saw that day he first set foot in Wonder. Before his large body, and even before his gleaming white straw fedora – which was wafted high above his head in greeting – there was Bruce's smile, immediately ingratiating him with all who bore witness.

The entire town, seventy including Nimble, gathered to make Bruce's acquaintance, and what a sight they must have been for the new arrival. But if Bruce was taken aback he didn't let on in the slightest. He just politely lifted his hat and let rip an absolute whopper of a smile, rotating his head every now and then to ensure everyone had had sufficient chance to bask in its warmth.

The crowd turned towards Francis, as founder of the town the implication seemed to be that he would lead the welcome procession.

Francis stepped forward and tried to offer, in Bruce's direction, a smile of his own, but so unremarkable a smile it was in comparison to what Bruce had just enveloped the townspeople in, it seemed more of an insult than a greeting. A tense silence followed as the crowd waited for Bruce's response, fearful lest this extraordinary smiling scarecrow feel offended.

The silence seemed to last for an eternity before it was suddenly broken by Bruce, who burst into a humongous belly laugh. "The name's Bruce," said Bruce. "Bruce Fella."

"Francis Wonder," returned Francis, breathing an internal sigh of relief that was simultaneously shared by the entirety of Magnificent Mert's Spectacular Circus.

Bruce was an architect. He had travelled the world and had designed some of the most famous buildings in civilised society, from unfathomable skyscrapers to entire cities. Respected though he was, however, Bruce had always dreamt of designing a city based around the idea of whimsy, rather than efficiency, but of course no government in the world would indulge his fantasies.

Thus Bruce arrived in Wonder, searching for a place where could realise his life's endeavour, and he truly could not have found a better place to do so.

Over the next few months he and Francis, and more often than not Mert, began to dream up the magical town that would one day become Wonder.

The discussions followed issues such as, what would be the most acrobatic route to the river? which part of the land feels the most mystical? and where would be best to locate "The Forest of Doom," for anyone seeking an intrepid quest?

10

The Arrival of Geronimo the Trickster

It's like the old Wonder saying goes: "You wait ages for a bus, and then a circus turns up." No one really knew what the saying meant.

But just like that, after the time Francis had spent with only Nimble for company, he was now inundated with guests, and the population of the town only continued to grow.

For it was not long after the arrival of Bruce, a momentous occasion in the history of Wonder, given his complete affability and the unconditional affection that everyone felt for him – not to mention the sacrifice he would later make for his beloved townspeople – that another peculiar traveller made his way through the tall grass and into the lives of Francis, Nimble, Bruce, and Magical Mert and his Spectacular Travelling (no longer) Circus.

If Bruce's arrival was the metaphorical equivalent of a cool glass of pink lemonade on a stiflingly hot summer's day, then the introduction of Geronimo into Wonder bore more resemblance to that of an ice cold raindrop quickly diving between your coat collar and the bare skin on your back on a day already cold enough to make the teeth of polar bears chatter.

The day was unusually dull for a day in Wonder, the sky not its usual pastel blue but more a languid porpoise colour, while the sun hid almost intentionally away behind an ominous black cloud, almost in anticipation of the new arrival. The townspeople agreed that the thunder and lightning was a bit much as Geronimo approached, but the weather in Wonder was nothing if not theatrical.

There was an air of trepidation, the oxygen around not its normal lucid self, but more claggy and difficult to digest, and, as the unfamiliar figure neared from over the horizon, a small crowd gathered to meet him.

In stark contrast to Bruce's ginormous frame, Geronimo was diminutive in size, about the height of a particularly stunted garden gnome, and he walked with a limp in his left leg. His posture was far from textbook, his backed arched over so his long, slender nose almost touched his knees as he walked. One overly large toe had burrowed its way out of his shoe and wiggled freely around as he hobbled lopsidedly towards the amassing congregation.

Fairly well accustomed to the exceptional looking, the people of Wonder we not perturbed by Geronimo's appearance. They were as welcoming as they had been with Bruce.

Geronimo introduced himself nervously.

"Good day, townspeople," he said. "My name is Geronimo. Geronimo the faithful."

Francis stepped forward and offered Geronimo a hand, which the small man clasped with both his tiny hands and shook mightily.

"Welcome to our small town," said Francis. "Could we offer you a glass of lemonade? You must be parched from your travels."

"Much obliged," replied Geronimo most courteously.

And so they led Geronimo to the saloon and they all drank lemonade and ate pretzels and introduced themselves one by one.

Francis invited Geronimo to stay in Wonder, and as luck, or coincidence, or if you are a little more of a believer, fate would have it, Bruce, along with the help of the rest of the town, had just finished work on their newest (and Bruce's first designed) house.

And would you believe it, Bruce had always been extremely fond of miniature models – train sets, cars, even miniature towns – and he had always wanted to design and build a house of much smaller proportion that he had ever been previously commissioned. The detailed and precise work of constructing each piece of the abode was entirely fascinating to him.

And thus it was that Geronimo arrived in Wonder on the very day of the completion of what was effectively a home made bespoke for himself. He was overjoyed when they led him to his front door.

ll

Enter the Cowboy

The people of Wonder are, by nature, not a suspicious people. They give the benefit of the doubt wherever humanly possible, but they do possess a certain ability to sniff out a decomposing aura. And whether brought on by himself or by misfortunes he had met with previously in his life, Geronimo did carry around with him a rotten aura.

It was on the fourth day of Geronimo's residency in the town that a new traveller arrived. Shifty and searching, and straddled atop a magnificent Appaloosa horse, this imposing man asked the first person he happened upon – which just so happened to be Bruce Fella, the smiling scarecrow – if a small, decrepit man had passed through in the last few days.

Never one to be overly suspicious, but also a firm believer in a protector of one's own flock, Bruce simply flashed a blinding smile at the intruding cowboy, his teeth glistening so brightly that even the horse had to overt its gaze. The man astride the horse clicked his spurs into the spotted sides of his brilliant beast and trotted slowly, menacingly, away.

Bruce followed the man and the horse with his eyes until they had disappeared over the horizon. He then turned on his heels and ran as fast as he could in the direction of Geronimo's dinky dwelling, grabbing Francis and Mert on his way.

An incessant rapping upon the tiny door stirred in Geronimo a foulness, and he greeted his visitors in a sullen mood.

When Bruce explained what had just happened, however, the tiny man's demeanour quickly altered; his eyes darting quickly from left to right, scanning the horizon. He clutched a small, shining object that was slightly protruding from his waistcoat pocket.

"Maybe we'd better come in and discuss what's going on," suggested Mert. But Geronimo just snapped a harsh "NO!" before slamming the minuscule door in their knees.

With no other option, it was decided that Francis, Bruce and Mert should retire to the saloon to discuss the events, and formulate a plan for the future. And it was as they were ordering a round of sarsaparillas that they noticed the visitor sat in the corner of the tavern, his Stetson tipped slightly over his eyes.

Francis ordered an extra sarsaparilla and the three of them made their way over to the cowboy's table.

"Howdy," said Mert, somewhat regretfully.

The cowboy raised his head ever so slightly and gave the three a scowl.

"Brought you a sarsaparilla," said Francis.

"Whiskey! Neat!" replied the cowboy.

"I think you'll find the sarsaparilla to your liking," said Bruce.

The cowboy sniffed at the bottle and took a swing, holding the neck between his two forefingers and his thumb, and before that first bubble had a chance to fizzle and pop on its way down his throat, there was a visible weight lifted from the shoulders of the cowboy. His lightness was suddenly palpable, his sullen demeanour so changed it was difficult to ever imagine him having been anything other than jovial.

"I haven't tasted sarsaparilla like that since I was a young buck," he said. "Me and my sister would swipe a bottle each from our old mam's saloon every weekend. Wow! That takes me back! Much obliged, gentlemen."

"Pleasure," smiled Francis.

"I've been chasing that damned garden gnome so fucking long I'd completely forgotten what it was to enjoy something, and enjoy it for enjoyment's sake!"

"And why are you chasing this 'gnome' character?" asked Bruce.

"Well," said the cowboy, "it's a bit of a tale. Pull up a pew if you're interested, but it's a pretty long story."

And so it was that Francis, Mert and Bruce came to find out the truth about Geronimo, how it was that he came to Wonder, and what it was that he was harbouring in his waistcoat pocket.

12

A Brief History of Geronimo, the Cowboy and the Magic Watch

This is the story that the Cowboy told Francis, Mert and Bruce over many more sarsaparillas.

"I come from a small town west of here. A ranching town. Was born and raised there, and my daddy before me was born and raised there. But his daddy, my grand-daddy, well, he was a wanderer.

He followed the stars all over this great, wide world, travelling by day, and by night, resting his head under the soft glow of the moon.

He never knew any other kind of life, and he travelled from town to town with his horse Buster, picking up work here and there, but mainly keeping to himself out on the plains.

He knew the calls of the wolves and the hyenas, and he knew their scent, so he knew where was safe to spend the night, and where he should quickly move on from.

One night, as he settled down to rest, Buster happily munching from his feed bag, a small man came by. He approached my grand-daddy and sat next to him on his blanket.

The small man has a mischievous kind of smile, and a devilish twinkle in his eye, and he asked my grand-daddy if he might borrow a small ladle of water for to quench his thirst.

Never being the stingy kind, my grand-daddy kindly offered him as much water as he liked, and told him he was free to spend the night on the blanket.

The small man accepted and made himself comfortable, also accepting a small supper of boiled corn from my grand-daddy.

Before they nodded off into slumber my grand-daddy enquired as to where the small man was travelling to, and the small man became agitated. He told him it was none of his business before rolling over and falling instantly asleep.

The next morning when my grand-daddy arose the small man, along with the remaining water and corn, were gone.

Never one to overreact, grand-daddy saddled Buster and headed for the nearest town to find a little work and restock on supplies.

When he arrived at the town however, he found a large crowd awaiting him, and just behind them was the small man.

"That's him!" cried the small man and the mob advanced towards my grand-daddy.

"What's going on?" asked grand-daddy.

"We don't take kindly to folks robbing poor, innocent folks like our little friend here," explained one of the angered crowd, and before grand-daddy had the chance to put the record straight they began hurling rocks at him and Buster. Grand-daddy fled.

That evening, hungry and thirsty, grand-daddy again settled himself beneath the stars. All of a sudden he saw a quite magnificent light and out of the light stepped a fox.

I ain't able to explain exactly how it happened, but the fox warned my grand-daddy of a small man and a watch. The fox explained that the small man desired the watch because it had a special power, but that the small man must not be allowed to obtain the watch. The fox was very adamant that my grand-daddy must find the watch first and never let the small man possess it. If he did almighty danger would ensue.

So it was that my grand-daddy set out in search of the magic watch. The tale as to how he did in fact reach the watch before the small man is a long one, and one for another time, but suffice to say that the small man was not best pleased.

The two travelled the world four times over, my grand-daddy trying to escape the clutches of the small man, and the small man desperately seeking the watch.

After four years of this cat and mouse game, my grand-daddy decided that enough was enough, that he would settle down somewhere and await the inevitable arrival of the small man, come what may.

So he found himself a ranch and he waited, breaking horses and raising cattle to keep himself in food and clothes.

One thing my grand-daddy never counted on, though, was that he would fall madly in love. My grand-mammy was a hired hand that came once a week to help clean the house, but from the first moment she stepped through the door they instantly fell for each other.

They were married and my grand-mammy gave birth to my daddy, who inherited the ranch after they both died at the age of a hundred and eight.

But before grand-daddy died, he passed the watch down to my daddy, and made him promise he would protect it with his life, that he would never let the small man get his hands on it.

Daddy promised, and just before he died himself last year he made me promise the same thing.

I kept the watch under my mattress and to be perfectly honest, I more or less forgot about it. No one ever came up to the ranch and I had certainly never seen any small man. Or at least I hadn't, until last week."

13

The Cowboy and Geronimo Have it Out

Just then the saloon doors swung open and there stood Geronimo, looking oddly ominous for his size, his shadow engulfing much of the room as his beady eyes settled on the Cowboy.

"You!" hollered the Cowboy. Geronimo stood grinning menacingly. "Where's the watch?" the Cowboy demanded.

"You will never see that watch again," said Geronimo. "It never belonged to you, it was always my destiny."

Francis, Bruce and Mert exchanged glances a couple of times, before leaping to their feet to mediate between the Cowboy and Geronimo, who were now face to face – or more accurately face to groin.

There was a tenuous scuffle transpiring as the Cowboy tried to grab at the impish man, but Geronimo was slippery, evading hands and feet and fingers and toes. For a while there was an almost comical pursuit as the Cowboy chased the exceptionally nimble Geronimo around the saloon; light shades were swung from, table tops were bounced on, balconies leapt from. Eventually though, Francis managed to grab a hold of Geronimo as he was parkouring his way from wall to wall, and Mert and Bruce manhandled the Cowboy into a wooden chair, facing his foe.

"Please help me," Geronimo pleaded with the Wonder-ites. "This Cowboy and his family have been trying to steal my watch for decades now. I thought I was finally safe in this town, but he has still found me. Will he not just let me be?"

The Cowboy scoffed and Francis asked Geronimo whether or not it was in fact he that had stolen the watch.

"Preposterous, sir," replied Geronimo. "Or my name isn't Geronimo the Faithful."

"Faithful?" the Cowboy sniggered. "This here is Geronimo the Trickster. The most deceitful imp this side of the hemisphere. I've heard all about you over this past week Geronimo. Each town you passed through since stealing my watch has had more than a few choice words to say about you."

"Don't listen to him," Geronimo implored. "He's just a crazy Cowboy."

"How about Brinsville, eh?" the Cowboy honed his gaze onto Geronimo, who's expression had suddenly altered.

"Yes," continued the Cowboy, "the town you burned to the ground right before arriving here."

There was an audible gasp around the saloon and Geronimo knew he was licked.

"Okay, okay," he said, "let me explain myself. Francis, could I please have a sip of your sarsaparilla? My throat is parched after being chased by this oaf." But as Francis turned to grab a glass, Geronimo threw a pinpoint elbow which sent his capturer reeling backwards and allowed the small man time enough to flee; the open top half of the window opposite the door was just large enough for him to leap through.

14

Geronimo is Foiled and the Watch
is Returned to the Cowboy

After escaping through the window Geronimo fled for his tiny house as fast as his little legs could take him. He was but a few feet from his front door when he felt a hand grab him by the shoulder and lift him into the air. Struggling to break free Geronimo flailed and mauled at his captor, but it was only when he had calmed down somewhat and turned to look behind him that he noticed it was not a person at all. Geronimo's coat lapel had snagged on a thick tree branch, and as his momentum had carried him skyward, there had the branch remained, holding Geronimo at least four feet off the ground.

Geronimo paddled his legs with desperation but he could not break free of the grasp of the tree, and this was the image presented to his pursuers, who had now quite significantly grown in number.

In fact, more or less the whole town was now present, and as Geronimo threatened, swore and abused, they all helped the Cowboy search for the watch.

They rifled through draws, they turned over mattresses, they peeled through keyholes and in wardrobes, and they even checked Geronimo's pockets; the tiny gremlin wailing as they did so – he was overtly ticklish.

"So what exactly is the deal with this watch?" Francis asked the Cowboy as they rummaged through a coffer.

"It's magic," replied the Cowboy.

"Yeah, so I've heard. But what exactly is 'magic' about it."

"Well," said the Cowboy, seemingly unsure if he should reveal the secrets of the watch to Francis. "Most watches track time and move forward, correct?"

"Right," affirmed Francis.

"Well this watch ticks backwards."

"Seems less a magic watch and more a useless watch to me."

"No, you see, it ticks towards the moment of death for whoever possesses it."

Francis was stunned for a minute. "You mean," he said, "it tells you when you're going to die?"

"Exactly," said the Cowboy.

"So why would it be so dangerous in Geronimo's hands?"

"I'm not sure. I only know that he should never be allowed to possess it completely. I suppose time is fragile and something like this could be used to manipulate the future, even if I don't know how."

This seemed so surreal and vague that it almost made perfect sense to Francis, who at that moment spotted something gleaming in the late afternoon sun. Taped to the top side of one of the roof beams something was attracting his attention, beckoning him with its luminous winking.

Francis hoisted himself up the beam and reached his hand around, feeling for the object. He grabbed the watch, pulled it free of the tape and dropped neither gracefully nor clumsily to his feet.

He opened his palm and he and the Cowboy both stared at the watch. The Cowboy made to grab for it.

"Hang on," Francis said as he snatched his hand away, protecting the watch. "How do we know that you're telling the truth, that the watch isn't actually Geronimo's and you are the one trying to steal it?"

The Cowboy thought for a moment, tugging at the front of his Stetson with his two forefingers as he did so. Finally he moved his hand to the back of his hat and pulled it backwards to reveal his face, which was now smiling at Francis.

"Tell you what," he said, "you keep the watch."

Francis looked at the Cowboy suspiciously. "How's that now?" he asked.

"Well," said the Cowboy, "I need to stop the small man from obtaining the watch, but I can still do that easily enough, perhaps more easily in fact, if you help me by looking after the watch. Particularly if you allow me to stay in your town."

It made sense in the way that only things in Wonder made sense, and so Francis agreed.

Thus it was that the Cowboy came to give up his ranch and move into a coincidentally – or not – newly built home in Wonder, compete with a pen for his Appaloosa horse; and so it was that Francis came into ownership of the magic watch, which he held in his palm with the knowledge that inside it contained the very instant that his death would occur. His desire to open the watch was matched only by his desire to never open the watch, a battle that would continue to rage in him for a good while yet.

As for Geronimo, well, he remained in Wonder also, but no longer in his tiny custom-built house. From that day on he remained where he was when crowd of pursuing townspeople had found him, lifted four feet from the ground by the oak tree just outside his former home.

15

How Francis and Annie Fell in Love

Annie's eyes were like no eyes Francis had ever seen before. Annie's eyes were a warm orange, atmospheric and entrancing. When she was angry they burned like a violent fire, and when she calmed they resembles two peaches, sweet and rich with vitamins.

Nimble loved the beach and he and Francis would spend hours there in the afternoons; playing fetch, chasing the tide, and sharing ice cream as they sat in the sand together. It was truly one of the happiest places in Francis's life.

It was this scene of man and dog sat side by side, watching the sun as it dipped cautiously into the sea, that made Annie's heart skip a little. It was the scene of them alternately licking a knickerbocker glory that made her stomach skip a little.

Annie also loved the beach, especially in the early evening. The golden sand was warm and soft and the sea breeze wrapped around her like a kimono.

She also especially loved the beach because it was the perfect opportunity to 'bump' into Francis and Nimble.

Since the day she had met Francis – when her timeline had momentarily evolved from its usual linear state and wrapped itself around her in such a way as to rearrange all she had ever previously believed possible – she had fallen head over heels in love with him.

She had no idea that he himself was dumbstruck with longing for her; she assumed he was unaware of her existence, or worse still, viewed her only as Mert's daughter.

That Francis and Nimble were nightly at the beach was not solely down to both of their love of sand and dunes. They came for Annie. Just to catch a glimpse of her was all Francis hoped for.

Finally tired of the nervous glances, the blushed cheeks, the hidden smiles, Nimble took it upon himself to take action. Though it is well remarked upon that dogs can smell fear, it is seldom known that love also has a distinctive scent to the canine family.

Nimble set off at full gallop, heading straight for Annie. Annie had been briefly introduced to Nimble on a couple of occasions but was by no means overtly familiar with his demeanour. So it was that when Nimble came charging towards Annie, teeth snarling and eyes ablaze, she turned and ran as fast as she could.

Nimble did not let up though, even through Francis's yells and pleads for him to "STOP!" and "HALT!" and "HEEL!" and even "SIT!"

Nimble chased Annie all over the beach, with Francis in hot pursuit behind. Eventually Annie ran out of beach and Nimble had her cornered. Francis approached behind and implored Nimble to stop, but the dog leapt forward and forced Annie into the sea.

Just as with fear and love, dogs also possess the extraordinary ability to smell the ability to, or not to, as the case may be, swim. Nimble was well aware that Annie could not breaststroke, backstroke or indeed even doggy paddle her way to dry land once she was engulfed in the ocean's thrumming waves.

It took Francis perhaps a little too long to realise what Nimble already knew, and it was only once Annie had disappeared from sight, slipping beneath the bobbing surf, that he dived to pull her to safety.

As she came to, Francis was over her and Nimble was licking her face, terrified he'd gone too far and caused a disaster.

That night they lay on the beach watching the moonlight dance across the waves, and it was when they woke in the morning, warm and safe in each other's arms, that they noticed Annie was visibly pregnant.

They spent the next nine months in complete enthral with each other, seemingly unable to physically let go of one another.

They spent their mornings watching dandelion fruits travelling on the wind. They spent their afternoons by the river, catching crayfish. And they spent their evenings dancing to the sound of the town.

Years later they would laugh in bewilderment at the gall of the mutt who had brought them together, whilst also cringing at the overtly clichéd and chivalrous way in which their souls were first properly intertwined. A damsel Annie was not, and Francis never thought himself particularly brave, though of course he was.

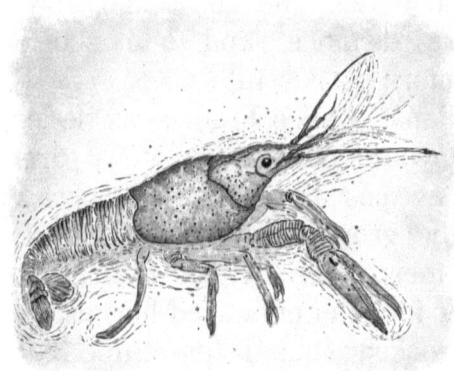

16

The Birth of a Wonder

It was exactly nine months from that night at the beach that Francis, Annie and Nimble were slouching languidly on the front porch of Francis's house, which Annie now also resided in.

As their eyes relaxed and the sunset turned into a hazy dream, Nimble pricked his ears and began to bark.

Appearing over the horizon, through the tall grass, were two silhouettes; one tall, remarkably well dressed, even from a distance, and one shorter, but more determined, more purposeful.

"Mama! Papa!" wailed Francis, as he leapt to his feet and rushed towards the outlines of his parents.

Nimble flew past Francis and toppled Margret Shelly Wonder to the ground, covering her face with canine saliva as Francis embraced his father, then helped his mother to her feet and embraced her also.

Francis looked behind for Annie but noticed she hadn't moved from her rocker on the porch. It was only when he squinted that he noticed her pronounced breathing, and he knew that their child about to enter the physical world through the most majestic portal of all.

Francis ran as quickly as he could back towards Annie, with his parents and Nimble in pursuit behind.

"Are you all right?" Francis asked.

"I think the baby's coming," replied Annie.

"Not to worry," interrupted Margret, "everything is going to be just fine."

"Annie," said Francis, "this is my mother, Margret. And this is Theodore, my dad."

"Pleased to meet you," Annie managed to squeeze out between contractions.

And so it was that Margret Shelly Wonder delivered her grandson into the world right there on the front porch of Francis and Annie's home, the moment washed a deep pink by the dipping evening sun. A most memorable occasion for all.

It wasn't long before word had spread and Mert, along with the vast majority of his Spectacular Circus, as well as Bruce, and the Cowboy, had made their way over to the front porch of Francis and Annie's home to welcome the newest edition to the town – even Geronimo bellowed a "congratulations" (though perhaps sarcastically so) from his oak tree.

There was warmth and good feeling all around. Bruce opened a case of sarsaparilla and another of pink lemonade and passed them round, while Francis held his newborn son in one arm and caressed Annie's hair with the other.

It was a miraculously simple birth, partly owing to Annie's inert flexibility after years of working in a circus, understudying the acrobats and whatnot, and partly due to Margret Shelly's expert midwifery skills – she had never had a difficult birth yet.

As such Annie was happy to welcome the town into this intimate moment, particularly her father, who cried in front of his daughter for the first time in his life – and seldom stopped thereafter (tears of joy it should be added).

Francis and Annie named their son Michel but only Nimble knew why. As he grew older, father and son loved to fish in Wonder's miraculous stream, a haven for some of the world's most seldom seen fish, fish who almost seemed to enjoy being caught.

More often than not Annie would join them. Francis had never fished before he came to Wonder, but in her previous life Annie had been a keen fisherwoman. She loved nothing more than wading in, waist deep, and spending the lazy summer afternoons with her rod in the water. She wouldn't be the least bit frustrated if she never had a bite all day – though she was actually a very successful fisher; it seemed as though, like humans, the fish were somehow drawn to her.

As Annie fished, Francis and Michel would idle beside the stream with their net, catching the crayfish.

So exotic did these crustaceans seem to Francis when he first arrived in Wonder that he never tired of scooping one up in his net and inspecting it thoroughly, watching each leg paddling back and forth while the claws snapped in derision. Francis would then gently lay the tiny lobster back in the stream and let it be swept away in the ripples of the current. These afternoons spent with Michel and Annie were among the most precious in Francis's life.

17

The Truly Wondrous Roads of Bruce Fella

The years passed in a blur of contentment following the birth of Michel. The population of Wonder grew week on week, month on month, until soon they were inundated with characters brimming with quaint, fanciful, eccentric and whimsical electricity.

The town was now a hub of life, and the structure put in place by Bruce, the houses, the roads, the communal areas, all pulled together to create a living environment like no other. For, as previously mentioned, Bruce's houses were bespoke: made for each individual or family that inhabited it. The house would reflect completely the personality of its residents, whilst also constantly astonishing its keepers with small surprises, surprises that somehow told them new things about themselves, surprises that unlocked doors inside them that they themselves did not even know were there, let alone under lock and key.

And Bruce's roads. Well, for those who never lived in Wonder, Bruce's roads are almost beyond description.

Bruce's roads were a tapestry of inventiveness and imagination. They were a promenade of beauty and majesty. And as to how they worked they remain a compete mystery.

For Bruce's roads did not stand idly by as most roads do. No, Bruce's roads never took you in the same direction more than once. Annoying, you may think, frustrating and infuriating even. But no, for Bruce's roads always took you to your desired destination.

Francis Wonder was a man full of imagination and whimsy, and in Bruce he had found not only a kindred spirit, but also a man with a remarkable ability to bring his marvels into existence. The two became inseparable, as close as brothers, and so it was that Bruce came to be a pivotal figure in the life of the Wonders, and in particular in the life of Michel, who he loved as his very own son.

18

Something Big Happens

Owing to Bruce's large reach, it was decided by Michel that the lovable scarecrow would be the perfect "catcher" to Michel's flying trapeze act.

The two worked tirelessly at the act and often put on performances for the town; of course all the equipment was readily available to Bruce and Michel owing to the (no-longer) travelling circus.

Being a town largely consisting of circus folks, Wonder would always bristle with encouragement at any form of acrobatic display, and the indulgence from the town in Bruce and Michel's semi-regular performances had become something of a tradition.

Bruce and Michel did incorporate nuances into their act, but mainly the Flying Trapeze was the showstopper.

It was three days before Michel's sixth birthday when something big happened. The town had gathered in the seats surrounding the outdoor circus ring that resided at the very centre of Wonder for another of Bruce and Michel's performances.

Bruce had been working on a juggling act, complete with skittles and eventually Michel himself, and he was neatly underway, warming up the crowd with tosses, catches, and the odd flash of his glittering smile.

It was while Bruce was launching his skittles from one hand to the other, incorporating a cat here and a mouse there, that something half buried in the sand caught Michel's eye. As inquisitive as any young child, he wandered over to inspect a little more thoroughly.

Of course Francis recognised it instantly. It was a military issue hand-grenade, the same model that had killed the men in his platoon all those years ago, in fact. Michel waved the pin above his head and gestured for his father to take a closer look at his discovered treasure, his other hand clutching the now live grenade.

Francis's heart began to best faster than it had ever done before. He set off running towards his son.

"FRANCIS, STOP!" shouted Bruce, who prised the grenade from Michel's fingers and held it tight to his chest. He bade Michel to run towards his father. Francis called his name and Michel ran, suddenly aware from the alarm in the voices of Bruce and his father that he was in danger.

As Michel reached his father he was engulfed in his arms. Francis shouted for Bruce to throw the grenade, but Bruce's figure had already begun to take on an opaqueness, and Francis knew there was nothing he could do.

There was nowhere that Bruce could throw the grenade that wouldn't endanger someone, surrounded as he was by the rest of the town.

The townspeople backed away tentatively. Francis pushed Michel towards Annie and tried to run to Bruce, but Annie caught his arm and held him in place, pulling him back into the crowd and into the safety of his family.

There was a deafening silence, a silence that lasted an eternity, then suddenly a light flashed that was so bright the townspeople were forced to avert their eyes. When they looked back, Bruce was gone, only blackened dust remained in the centre of the circus ring, where we had stood clutching the grenade tightly to his chest.

A sadness that was beyond all previous sadness descended upon Wonder. The town openly wept for the scarecrow who had done so much for all of them. And to this day, no one is really sure if the blinding light they saw that fateful afternoon came from the grenade, or whether it came from Bruce, the smiling scarecrow, smiling his final smile on this earth.

19

The End

Francis's eyes filled with tears as he saw the people of his life approaching from over the horizon and through the tall grass, the pink sun draping the moment in its warmth. His head was filled with thoughts, thoughts and questions.

His overriding emotion was gratitude. Francis was aware of just how extraordinarily his life had been, so full of excitement, adventure, and above all love. His soul sat beside him in the form of the most beautiful freckle-adorned woman he had ever met, with his son adding to his life a joy he had never dreamed to imagine.

With his bountiful family surrounding him, Francis wondered whether the figures approaching were real or apparitions. No longer were the dead opaque, they were solid and defined. Did this mean Francis himself was dead? He held out a hand in front of his eyes, but he could not see through it. But what did that mean if he couldn't see through the others, either?

Where am I? he thought. What is this place we have made? Is it real? Was it ever real? He looked at Annie, who, knowing as she always did, placed her hand atop Francis's. She smiled at him, a knowing smile, as she had done all those years ago.

It was then that Francis felt the heaviness of the Cowboy's watch in his inside breast pocket. He knew it was time to open it. But what would it say? Would the time be now? Or had Francis's time already been and passed? Was this already paradise?

He took the watch from his pocket and steadied his trembling hand, Annie squeezing his other. Francis looked at the watch, the sun reflecting on its now rusted encasing. He popped open the lid to reveal the dial. He took a deep breath, exhaled and let his eyes drift down to the watch face, but as his eyes focused he realised that there were no hands on the watch.

Epilogue

Countless scholars, academics, philanthropists, entrepreneurs, psychologists, psychiatrists, mystics, gurus, optimist and pessimists have debated the existence of Wonder for many years.

Some deny its existence, some accept its existence in an existential sense, a subject on which many an academic paper has been written, some believe that it did at one time exist in a real and physical form, and some even insist that Wonder did and in fact still does exists.

A large proportion of this latter group have devoted their lives to finding Wonder, searching the globe over for a man with a raft that will take them through the swampland and out into the crystal clear water, onto the land where the animals sing, and through the tall grass, backdropped as ever by the warming pink sun, where they will be greeted by acrobats, lion tamers, fortune tellers, clowns, mimes, trapeze artists, sword swallowers, fire eaters, tightrope walkers, ventriloquists, ventriloquist's dummies, a most magnificent ringmaster, a friendly cowboy, a disgruntled gnome in a tree, and a smiling scarecrow, and of course a man, woman, child and dog whose dreams intertwine with everyone they meet, to build up the magnificent and wondrous world around them, a world that can take your innermost desires and turn them into, if not quite reality, then the closest thing you will ever need.

As of yet no one has managed to find the Town of Wonder.

www.ingramcontent.com/pod-product-compliance
Lightning Source LLC
Chambersburg PA
CBHW051713180726
48283CB00004B/1328